PUSS IN BOOTS

ILLUSTRATED BY
EDMUND MORIN

RETOLD BY JOSEPHINE POOLE

HUTCHINSON

LONDON · MELBOURNE · AUCKLAND · JOHANNESBURG

There was once a miller who earned much, and spent much, so that when he died he left nothing but his mill, his ass, and his cat. He had three sons. The eldest moved into the mill, the second took the donkey; but the youngest got only the cat.

He sat down in a field and groaned aloud. 'What will become of me?' he cried. 'It's all very well for my brothers! If they work together they are set up for life, but what can I do with a cat? Even if I eat him, and make gloves of his fur, I shall soon be hungry again. I am afraid I shall starve to death.' And the poor fellow's eyes filled with tears.

Then up spoke the cat, and the strange thing was that the young man could understand every word he said. 'My dear master, if you must shed tears, weep for your lamented parent, and try not to be cast down by appearances. As you see, I am only a cat, but if you will make me a pair of boots, so that I can scamper through dirt and brambles without hurting my soft paws, you may find that you have the best of the bargain.'

The young man was touched by this speech, and felt suddenly hopeful, for in the past he had often admired the cleverness of this cat, and the many cunning ways he had of catching rats and mice. So he obtained a pair of little leather boots, as well as a strong drawstring bag that the animal asked for.

Mr Puss pulled on the boots, which fitted him exactly. Then he put some bran and some sprigs of sow thistle into the bag, and crept away into the thickest part of the hedge. Here he arranged his bag so that the opening gaped wide, and stretching himself out beside it, he lay quite still, as if he were dead – but all the time he held on to the strings of the bag with his forepaws.

It was not long before a silly rabbit hopped up, and fearfully examined the cat – but he did not move a whisker. Next the rabbit began poking about the bag, to see what it contained. It smelt nice. By and by, he ventured in. Puss drew the strings in a trice, and the rabbit was a prisoner; he killed him, heaved him up on his shoulder, and set off at once for the palace.

It was a very hot day, and the way was long and dusty. But the cat trudged on, until at last he arrived at the gate. He told the guard that he wanted to speak to the King, and he was shown upstairs to His Majesty's apartment.

He laid down the rabbit in front of the King, and made a low bow. 'Sire,' said he, 'I come from my lord the Marquis of Carabas.' This was the title he had invented for his master. 'He desires me to present you with this rabbit from his warrens, with his greetings and best wishes.'

The King was somewhat astonished, but answered politely with his thanks to the Marquis. And the cat went away.

Next time he went out very early, and hid with his bag in a cornfield until he caught some partridges. These too he presented at the palace, and the King was pleased, and after this he often received game from the Marquis.

It happened that the King went out driving with his daughter, the most beautiful princess in the world. The cat ran at once to his master, and said, 'Go to the river, take off your clothes, and jump in! Ask no questions, but do what I say, and your fortune is made!' And he scampered after, and took his master's clothes and hid them under a stone. Then he saw the royal carriage, and began to shout, 'Help! Help for the Marquis of Carabas! Robbers have stolen his clothes, and left him to drown!'

The King ordered his guards to rescue the young man. He took him into his carriage, and lent him a suit from the royal baggage. Then the boy looked so handsome that the Princess immediately fell in love with him. The three drove on together.

But the cat ran ahead, and found some reapers out in the fields. 'When the King passes you must pretend that all this belongs to the Marquis of Carabas,' he ordered. 'Otherwise I will make mincemeat of you!' They were so frightened that they obeyed him.

At last the cat came to a great castle, which belonged to a wicked ogre. He was exceedingly rich, and owned all the fields of hay and corn along the road. He also possessed a magic power, for he could turn himself into any shape he wanted.

But Mr Puss had found out all about him, and what he could do. So he darted into the castle, and leapt up the stairs to the very top, where he found the ogre sitting alone in a little room, drinking beer. They exchanged greetings, and the ogre was as polite as it was possible for him to be, though he looked at the cat now and then with greedy eyes, as though he might fancy to make a meal of him.

'I have heard many tales of the marvellous shapes you can change yourself into,' began the cat, trying not to shiver. 'They say you can become a lion, or an elephant, or a bear, whenever you like, but really I can't believe it.'

The ogre roared, and dashing his mug of beer upon the ground, instantly changed into a lion, which so alarmed poor Pussy that he fled, hissing and spitting, out of the window, and scrambled to safety over the gutter as fast as he could in his boots.

Then the ogre resumed his natural shape, and the cat came down, still trembling.

'That gave you a fright!' rumbled the ogre, with a cruel grin. And he slapped his great thigh.

'So it did,' said the cat, trying to keep his voice steady. 'I admit you have partly convinced me—'

'What do you mean?' bellowed the ogre, and his small eyes burned red with rage.

'You are big and fierce, and you turned yourself into something that is also big and fierce. Perhaps that isn't so difficult to do! I think it might be very much harder for you to change into something little and helpless – a mouse, for instance.'

No sooner said than done. The ogre vanished with a roar that dwindled into a squeak, and a tiny grey mouse scuttled across the floor. Puss pounced – and gobbled him up!

Next moment he heard carriage wheels running over the drawbridge.

The King had noticed the ogre's fine castle as he was driving past, and decided to pay him a vist. The cat was just in time to greet him in the courtyard. 'Welcome to the home of my lord the Marquis of Carabas,' he said, with a deep bow.

The King looked about, impressed with the splendour of every-thing. The cat led the way into the banqueting hall, where a feast was waiting for the ogre's friends; but seeing that the King was there, they did not dare to enter. The King sat at the head of the table, with his daughter and the miller's son on his right and left, while Puss stood upon a stool. The ogre's servants passed the dishes, and poured the wine, but the Princess and the young man did not eat much, only looked lovingly at each other. And really the King was delighted with his host the Marquis, his refined manners, and handsome figure.

'You have rich estates, my Lord, and a splendid castle,' he said at last, as the butler filled his glass for the sixth time. 'I'll speak plainly! I can see that my daughter is head over ears in love, and for my part, I'll be glad to have you as my son-in-law.'

So the blushing young man took the most beautiful of princesses for his bride, and the wedding was celebrated that same afternoon.

As for the cat, he was made a Lord, and never chased mice any more, except for his own amusement.

First published in 1988
by Hutchinson Children's Books
An imprint of Century Hutchinson Ltd
Brookmount House, 62-65 Chandos Place,
Covent Garden, London WC2N 4NW

Century Hutchinson Australia (Pty) Ltd
16-22 Church Street, Hawthorn, Melbourne,
Victoria 3122

Century Hutchinson New Zealand Limited
32-34 View Road, PO Box 40-086, Glenfield,
Auckland 10

Century Hutchinson South Africa (Pty) Ltd
PO Box 337, Bergvlei 2012, South Africa

Set in Goudy Old Style by
The Graphic Unit, London

Designed by ACE limited

Printed and bound in Italy

British Library Cataloguing in Publication Data

Morin, Edmund
    Puss in Boots. — (Golden classics).
    I. Title   II. Poole, Josephine   III. Perrault
    Charles. Chat Botte   IV. Series
    823'.914[J]   PZ7
    ISBN 0-09-172708-1